Ember Sparks

An Anthology of Themes

Sasha Nguyen

Beaverton, OR

2010

Copyright © 2010 Sasha Nguyen
Cover Art Copyright © 2010 Maggie Forslund
All rights reserved under International and Pan-American
Copyright Conventions.

To all my dear family and friends to whom I have sometimes neglected over the years as I write. Thank you!

Table of Contents

Introduction .... pg 8

2007

Chase .... pg 16
Belief .... pg 24

2008

Utopia .... pg 46
Love .... pg 70
Blind Faith .... pg 88
Courage .... pg 98

2009

Umbrella .... pg 122
A Moment in Time .... pg 128
Sin .... pg 136

Tipsy .... pg 138

Treasured .... pg 142

2010

Obsessed .... pg 146

Victory .... pg 156

Dangerous Territory .... pg 160

Price .... pg 203

Shape-Shifting .... pg 210

Introduction

Life can be but a fleeting memory. Similarly, the time spent is but a short one. Though one's time may be brief, each moment is precious. To waste a single drop of that time is to step further into regret. But time wisely spent can be the greatest of treasures.

Speaking of regret, it's painful. To have knowledge that a single action could have changed the outcome could hurt as much as a physical wound.

I do not want to live in regret. I will admit that I am only human and mistakes will be made, but I want to seek a path in life in which regret need not be a hindrance to me. Even if life becomes difficult, I can be content without regrets.

As such I started this anthology because I thought that creating a collection of my own short stories would be an absolutely great idea. Writing has always been my favorite thing to do, and I've always wanted to have a book out there with my name on it, so I decided I would go ahead and get that collection put together.

As I worked on this anthology, which has been in my thoughts for the past few months, I realized that this is truly a treasure that I will keep throughout the years. Even when my skill as a writer matures, I know that I will treasure it. To me, memories are precious and to have my past writing documented allows me to always remember the feelings I had when I wrote those stories.

And so, though it may be brief, it is my hope those feelings are conveyed through what I wrote. Enjoy~

Ember Sparks

2007

Chase

Halsie smiled cheerfully as she looked outside. The weather was bright and sunny, not a cloud in sight. All in all, it was a warm and wonderful day. A perfect day to draw was her thought as she walked away from the window. Sure, it was odd considering the constant autumn weather Renon sported, but frankly she didn't care. Why puzzle over odd weather when she could be out there drawing the wonderful sights?

Still grinning, Halsie reached down and grabbed her bag from the wooden corner of the bed. It contained everything she could possibly need while she was out. She carried it everywhere, no matter the place. She settled it firmly over her head and across one shoulder before going out of her room.

Her mother was in the kitchen as Halsie came in to grab a quick snack.

"Oh, morning dear," she greeted. "Off to the forest again?"

"Of course! It's warm, it's sunny, there's no way I'm going to miss out on this opportunity to enjoy it! Who knows, maybe I'll see something exciting today," Halsie said with a shrug. She waved goodbye to her mother and took a snack before she ran out the door.

Wow, it really was a beautiful day. There were so many forest creatures out as well. It was the perfect day for an artist!

Halsie sat down on a rock and took her bag off. Setting it down beside her, she began to take out her sketchbook when she noticed something peculiar.

There was a rabbit in front of her, a giant one at that. Its size wasn't what made it peculiar though. The fact that it was laying eggs was the main oddity. Plus, the eggs had weird designs on them. What the heck was up with this rabbit?!

"Hello, now that's weird," she mumbled.

The rabbit then hopped over to her and handed her one of its eggs.

Taking it, Halsie suddenly shouted in surprise as a loud explosion sound came from the egg and smoke poured out. She couldn't see though the white smoke and her ears were still ringing, so when the rabbit came thumping her way she had no idea of its approach. Without her knowledge, it had in one quick move swiped her bag and made its escape.

The smoke started to clear and her ears began to stop ringing as well. Looking around, Halsie's amber eyes widened as she saw what the rabbit had done.

Her bag was stolen and by a rabbit no less! What was up with that white ball of fluff? It was going to pay the second she got her hands on it. No rabbit was going to steal from her!

With a growl, Halsie shot to her feet and took off in the direction that the rabbit had left in. She probably wouldn't have known where it went if not for the eggs that had dropped.

She took care not to touch the eggs as she had learned the hard way that what came out was definitely not to be admired. Breaking the egg caused it to explode in a large splash of brown glop. There was still some of that sticky mess in her auburn colored hair. Hopefully she would be able to get it out once it dried, because there was no way she was stopping if that rabbit was still on the loose!

Speaking of the fluff ball… there it was! Halsie ran even faster as she saw the rabbit try to get away. It seemed to be teasing her as it hopped, shaking that fluffy tail before her eyes. How dare it? Whoever said that rabbits were docile and compliant was dead wrong! When she got her hands on that rabbit… it was dead!

The furry creature led her on a wild chase all the way under the roots of a large tree. Halsie clambered down to her knees as she crawled through. She came out through to the other side and immediately searched for the thief. She found it sitting innocently on a tree stump with her bag at the base.

"Why you... rabbit?" Halsie trailed off as she finally saw where she was. She was in a meadow with vibrant flowers of every color imaginable, and small streams flowed through the area. She looked behind the rabbit and saw a lake that glistened in its purity. "This... this is amazing."

The rabbit clearly agreed with her for it reached into her bag and pulled out her sketchbook. It gestured to her and she came over and took it.

"You want me to draw a picture of you?" she asked kneeling down to the rabbit's level.

The rabbit nodded and hopped back onto the tree stump before striking a pose with its tail poised in front of its face.

Halsie laughed as she reached into her bag to get out her drawing supplies. "You're a showy little rabbit aren't you?"

The rabbit merely responded with a twitch of its tail.

She smiled as she settled back. The fact that a rabbit lead her to a mysterious beautiful meadow was odd, but she would take it in stride. No use wasting a sunny wonderful day after all.

Belief

It was nearing Halloween, and the weather was still warm. Halloween was going to be a good one this year, I thought. I walked under a tree and laughed as leaves fell around me. I loved autumn, truly I did. The changing leaves, the crisp fall air, and the warm colors; it was really just wonderful.

The school bell rang and I hurriedly walked to school. Autumn was my favorite season, but I didn't want to be late because of it!

"Have you seen the new kid Fable?"

I looked up from eating my sandwich and shook my head. I finished the food in my mouth and asked, "No, I haven't. Why?"

"He is oh so *hot*!" Kathleen, Kat for short, gushed. She tended to be rather boy-crazy and she was also the only one in my group of friends who called me by my full name. I didn't know why, and when I had asked she answered saying that she thought it was cuter that way. I don't understand her sometimes.

"Kat's right. The new guy is hot, and then some," Brooke added on my right.

I glanced at her in surprise. Brooke never complimented a guy before! "Wow, this guy must be scorching hot then if you're commenting," I said taking another bite of my sandwich.

Brooke merely shrugged. "I'm just acknowledging the truth. I had him in my homeroom class. Looks alone, he seems to be your type Faye." She took a bite of her own lunch which happened to be a blueberry-flavored bagel.

"My type? What exactly is my type anyway if you think you know it so well?" I asked raising an eyebrow.

"You like the mysterious types that are taller than you. You also like them to be older than you and have fair blue eyes as well," Kat listed methodically counting them off on her fingers.

A twitch grew in my eyes as I said, "If you two know me so well, then why don't you go take my math test for me?"

"Next period? Sorry can't. I've got APUSH, and you know how much I LOVE that class," she said sarcastically, though a smile was on her face as she said it. I think she secretly loved that class; she just had to in order to have an 'A'. The faker, I thought with an inward grin.

"I have AP Chem.," Brooke said as she saw me look her way with pleading eyes.

"You people with your advance placement classes suck!" I whined getting rid of my look instantly. "If you didn't have it, you'd be in Algebra II with me to help me out in my misery and woe!"

"You'll survive, especially if you're able to describe yourself in such an amusing way," Brooke said finishing her lunch. She got up and threw it away. She came back and said, "You don't need our help Faye, you're good at math. You'll get through."

I nodded reluctantly and finished my lunch as well. "That doesn't mean I don't want help. Victory is sweeter when it is gained through less than legal ways," I told them.

"Yeah, yeah, whatever," Kat said waving her hand nonchalantly at what I said. "Look, the non-existent bell is going to ring soon, so I'm heading out." She waved goodbye at us before she left.

"Looks like it's just us now," I commented absentmindedly.

"Not really," Brooke said disagreeing with me with a small shake of her head. "I'm leaving too." She then walked off in the same direction as Kat, but not before giving one last amused smile at me.

I had only one question in my head as they were leaving. "Why am I always the one being left behind?" I whined before I left for my next class as well.

Despite all my complaining about my classes, I'm actually doing fairly well in them. Well, more than fairly well actually. I've got all A's and honors in my main classes.

The algebra test, I knew I was going to ace it. I didn't have to be a psychic to know **that**. Teachers often ask me why I don't just move into a higher class, but I always tell them that I don't feel the need to. What's the point anyway? I was only going to school for necessities sake. If I had wanted to, I could skip grades all the way to my senior year, and I was only a sophomore.

I was smart sure, but there are probably smarter people out there.

I sat down at my desk and took out my sketchpad. Class wouldn't start for another five minutes, so I doodled while I waited.

The teacher hadn't come in yet, so when the door opened I glanced up with an attentive look in preparation. The person I saw was actually much more interesting, not to mention drop dead gorgeous in his appearance. I didn't remember seeing him before, so I assumed he had to be the new guy. They're right, I thought. He is hot, fiery hot.

He looked around the room and stopped when he saw me. He started walking towards me and I felt my heart leap in my chest.

He was coming towards me. Me! What had I done to warrant his attention? I didn't have anything weird on my face did I? I was saved from imagining any weird scenarios when he stopped in front of my desk. "Hi," I said, and instantly a feeling of pride swept over me. I was able to talk to him without saying or acting weird at all! "I'm Fable Lennings."

"Hi, I'm Kale McCowen," he said his voice sounding as heavenly as he looked. "I saw you admiring the falling leaves this morning."

"You did?" I asked a blush coming onto my face. "I really love autumn. Do you?"

"Yeah, it's a nice season," he said smiling. His smile was amazing, I thought absently. "By the way, you have a ghost following you."

He's amaz— what?!?

"Uh... excuse me?" I asked my eyes shocked wide.

"I said you have a ghost following you," he repeated.

"Are you kidding me?" I asked frowning. I could not believe what I was hearing!

"No, I'm not. I never kid about these things," he said frowning as well. "Do you want to know about your ghost?"

I was saved from having to answer when the bell rang and people starting to file in. Kale went to sit down, reluctantly might I add, and I sighed. Why did I always have to like the weird ones?!?

The teacher came in and class immediately started. He briefly introduced Kale before passing out the tests. I took the paper he handed me and glanced at it; all simple questions, nothing hard at all.

I took out my pencil and breezed through the test. I just couldn't get how a cute guy like Kale had to be so weird! It just didn't seem fair… to me!

I mean the last crush I had turned out to be a loser and landed in juvenile hall. Now this one was a weirdo! I had no luck seriously.

"Wait up Fable!" Kale yelled as I was walking home.

"Why should I?" I asked without bothering to stop.

"Uh, because I asked?" he answered hesitantly in a questioning voice.

"Just because you asked doesn't mean I'll comply," I said dryly.

He shrugged and said, "So, do you want to know about the ghost that's following you?"

"No, now go away," I snapped annoyed at him. "There are no such things as ghosts anyway."

"Of course there are!" he argued indignantly. "They're everywhere if you could see them."

I decided to play along with him until he went away. At least then he might not act so annoying.

"Then I'm glad that I can't see them," I said with a snort.

"Ah, but some are pretty amazing!" Kale burst out enthusiastically. "Anyway, you really should know why your ghost is following you."

"No, I don't want to know," I argued in a deadpan voice.

"But you have to! You have to know!" he yelled in an almost desperate voice. Why the desperation I didn't know.

"Too bad, I don't want to," I said with a non-caring shrug. "Now leave me alone, my house is right here."

"Are you really sure about that? Maybe I should come with you!" he offered.

I stiffened. As hot as this guy was, he was way too crazy for my tastes. "No, absolutely not," I said before I pushed him away and walked into my home. I then locked the door and closed the curtains.

With a sigh I kicked off my shoes and collapsed onto the sofa. Boys were exasperating. I couldn't see how Kat dealt with them all the time. I closed my eyes as I tried to rest from the events of the day.

Suddenly I felt a cold draft on my face and I opened my eyes intent on getting rid of the problem. A scream burst from my throat as the face of my old boyfriend loomed over me. "Derek, what are you doing here? You're supposed to be in juvie!"

He smiled and I suddenly noticed how cold he felt. I scrambled off of the sofa and he seemed to drift away from me.

"What's wrong with you? Why are you so cold?" I asked. He started to approach me and I grabbed a fire stoker from its stand. I waved it at him as he continued to walk towards me. "Stay away!"

Derek didn't heed my words as he walked straight through the stoker. My scream died in my throat as I realized that Kale had been right about ghosts all along. They were real, and the very one following me had been my former crush!

The stoker fell from my hands as I backed away from him. He was a mere inches away from me and I gasped as I backed into the wall. "Get away from me!" I screamed as Derek started to reach for me with his pale hands. "Please, somebody help me!"

Just as I was beginning to think all was lost, I heard my window shatter and looked over to see Kale jumping through. "Fable, close your eyes!" he yelled as he reached into the bag he was holding.

I did just as Derek was a second away from touching me. The cold air that he exuded suddenly disappeared as I was pelted with small hard, round objects. I was breathing heavily as I leaned against the wall. "Kale, can I open my eyes now?"

"Yeah, go ahead," he answered.

I looked at the ground first to see small white pebbles. "Is that salt?"

"Yeah, ghosts don't tend to stick around after they're bombarded by those," Kale said as he looked around and after a moment settled his eyes on me. "You okay?"

I nodded. I was still scared, but I was all right. "Thanks for saving me, even after I was pretty rude to you."

He grinned and shook his head. "It's fine, I get that kind of reception a lot. Comes with the job."

"That's kind of a weird job to have, but I'm not complaining," I said grinning back. It faded though when a thought occurred to me. "But, is he gone for good? Or do I have to bring salt everywhere with me from now on?"

"Well… it would probably be a good idea to bring salt with you. He'll be back unless I can get him exorcised properly."

Great, my future was looking pretty grim.

"Is there anything I can help with? After all, the sooner that you do that, the sooner I'm safe right?" I asked with a weak grin.

"Well, as of this moment, you can help me with a place to stay," Kale suggested.

I blinked at him. "How can you not have a place to stay?"

"Because hotels are expensive, and I'm not very enthusiastic about explaining my parent-less situation to rent a room in the first place," he said wryly.

"You don't live with your parents?" I asked.

"No, I don't. So about that room…"

I thought it over as I looked at him. Inviting someone I had just met to stay at my home for an indefinite amount of time seemed like a crazy idea, but there was some good in it. He knew all about ghosts and how to handle them. If he stayed, I would have better protection. I bit my lip once before I nodded. "You can stay, but you're going to have to get permission from my parents yourself."

"I can do that," Kale said smiling. "Any other requirements?"

I narrowed my eyes as I came up with another one. "Can you teach me this ghost hunting business of yours? I mean, if they're actually real and all, I'd love to know more about them. As added protection and all," I explained.

"I can do that too. Anything else princess?" Kale asked teasingly.

I blushed and shook my head. "No, that's it. Um… thanks for saving my life."

"My pleasure," he said. He looked to the window and chuckled. "Now, how are we going to explain the window?"

Whoops, I had completely forgotten about that fact. I walked over to where the glass shards were and examined them. "I'll explain to my parents that some kids were playing baseball down the street and the ball hit the window."

"Well then, that settles that," Kale said. "When will your parents be coming home?"

"In a few hours," I answered after glancing at the clock on top of the television. "Help me clean this stuff up?"

"Sure, I caused the mess anyhow," he said. "Just direct me to the vacuum."

"Thanks," I said smiling at him. I went over to the closet and grabbed the vacuum along with a dust pan. I handed him the vacuum and went to work on the glass shards on the ground.

"What's your opinion on this? Do you think everything will work out?" Kale asked as he took off the cord of the vacuum cleaner.

I was pretty sure everything would work out okay. I believed that it would, and if there was anything that I've learned after today… belief is a powerful tool.

"Yes," I said after a moment. "I do believe it will."

2008

Utopia

His fingers flew across the keys as his eyes strained to read and reread the familiar language on the screen. Everything had to be perfect. Not one line, not one command could be wrong. It had to be just right, just perfect. Nothing could go wrong. Nothing, he thought as he paused to take a swig of water from the bottle next to his computer.

He turned around to look at a screen on the wall and stared blankly at the moving figures. They appeared to always be in a mood of perpetual happiness, or perhaps it was a mood of contentment. Nothing appeared to be wrong, but then that was the way that he had programmed it. His program, a world of idealism, called Utopia.

He put his bottle of water down and placed a hand on his chin in thought. There was something missing though. He just couldn't place what it was. The graphics were as they should be, as were the designs of the people. Could it be the world as a whole? Could it be that Utopia wasn't the ideal society that he had made it to be?

Impossible.

That could not be the reason.

He shook his head and turned away from the screen. He paused as he moved to go back to his desk. Though it clearly seemed impossible, could it be the reason?

He groaned and placed a hand on his forehead. The seeds of doubt had been sown, and he would not be able to continue until he was assured that his program was perfect.

How to test it though? He of course could not test it himself. He would need for someone to go into the program and experience the world. Who could possibly do that though? Who could he possibly trust to do an important task?

A knock on the door a room away made his eyes widen and he looked over to the monitor showing a feed of the front door. A broad grin appeared on his face as he found his answer. He made his way to the door and opened it still smiling. "Good evening Emi would you like to come in?" he asked gesturing her inside.

Emi smiled and walked inside. She took off her shoes and went to sit down comfortably on the sofa. She turned to face him and the smile slid off her face.

Though he was anxious to get his test underway, he was also curious as to the serious expression on his friend's face. He sat down as well and waited for her to speak.

It took her a moment as she appeared to collect her thoughts before she began to speak. "Jesse, there's something you need to know."

"Hm?" He raised an eyebrow urging her silently to continue.

Emi's eyebrows furrowed together and her hands came together in fists on her lap. She closed her eyes briefly before opening them again. He could see that she was about to speak and he focused his entire attention on her. "I'm having a hard time saying this, so I'm just going to spit it out. My landlord went bankrupt and he had to get rid of the entire complex. That means I have to move since I've got nowhere else to go. I was going to leave tonight, but I wanted to tell you first," she said quickly.

His thoughts about wanting a test subject fell away as he heard the news that his friend was telling him. "You can't move," he said immediately. "There has to be some other option!"

"There isn't," she said shaking her head. "I would have liked to stay in this town, but the only money I have on me has to go to getting me to my parent's place where I can crash for a bit until I have enough money to get another apartment."

Jesse glanced out the window and saw Emi's car filled with brown moving boxes. She couldn't move… she just couldn't. He closed his eyes and tried to think of a way that she could stay. A moment later he opened them a grin on his lips at his sudden idea. "Emi, you don't have to move."

She looked at him in frustration. "Haven't you been listening? I have to move! I have no other choice!"

"You do have a choice. I'll let you stay at my place until you can earn enough money to find a new apartment," he told her with a smile on his face.

"Really? You'd do that?" she asked her eyes aglow with sudden hope. "Wait, there's a catch isn't there?"

"Of course! Are you willing to partake in a test to secure your right to live at my home for an indefinite amount of time?" he asked her smiling still.

Her eyes narrowed before she nodded hesitantly. "I'm desperate, so fine. Now, what test is it?"

Jesse stood up and gestured for her to get up as well. "You'll see Emi dear; you'll soon see exactly what test it is."

"When you said test, I didn't realize you were going to hook me up to some program of yours. This isn't like that movie you know. You can't just make artificial worlds and hook people up as if they're lab rats," Emi protested though it was clearly in vain as she could see that her friend did not care. He was bent on perfecting his Utopia program and no words of protest from her would reach him now. Perhaps she should have refused to begin with.

"I know, but this clearly isn't going to be like that. For one, the world there was a dystopia, mine is a utopia hence the name," Jesse said fondly.

She frowned but kept quiet with her complaints nonetheless. She had already agreed, so she might as well not complain. "So, how is this going to work anyway? Because if this involves sticking needles into me at all… I'm out."

"Oh not to worry, there are no needles whatsoever. Those lines I placed on the side of your head will propel your subconscious into Utopia. You'll appear as if you are asleep, but your mind shall be wandering my program searching for anything not right," he told her as he made some final adjustments to the coding.

"I don't see why you need someone to go inside though. Couldn't you just check manually or something?" she asked trying not to move her head too much lest she remove the lines sticking to the side of her head.

"No, because the language is correct, but there is something missing. I am not sure what, that is another reason why I want you to go in there," he told her.

"Just a question, there aren't any reasons why I would be killed in there right?" Emi asked.

"As long as you do not give reason to," he said. "Now get ready, it is about to begin."

"Wait reason? What do you mean by that?" she cried before her eyes widened as the edges of her vision started to turn black. "Jesse!"

"You'll be just fine Emi, just fine," she heard before her vision turned entirely black and her world left her.

Emi opened her eyes and kept them wide open as she took in her surroundings. She was in a neighborhood where every house was the same and every lawn was the same. It was the same of everything!

All that she could see didn't seem possible, but as it was Jesse's program, of course it was possible.

She started walking forward and marveled at the fact that it actually felt like she was completely in the program. She smiled at that and had to admit that despite his odd moments, Jesse was certainly a genius with technology.

She had to focus though. Jesse had told her to look for something that seemed wrong or seemed missing. What could that look like though? She didn't know, so her only option was to continue walking.

It seemed like she had been walking for hours and she was growing drowsy with the sameness of everything. She was jolted out of her drowsiness when Jesse's voice erupted into the air.

"Can you hear me Emi? Of course you can hear me, I've programmed it to be able to put my voice in here," he said smugly.

"Can you hear me though?" she asked.

He didn't answer and she assumed that he could not hear her. It was while she stood waiting for Jesse to speak again did she see the gray square block coming towards her.

It rolled to a stop in front of her and she stared at it curiously. It grew in size and a thin red light appeared from it to shine on her. "You have violated code 3957, explain your reason before my timer gets to 0 or you shall pay the consequences," it said as the red light turned into two digits; 10.

Emi's eyes widened and she yelled, "Jesse! Help me out of here!"

He still couldn't hear her and she started to feel the first tendrils of panic. She had a flash back of what Jesse had said with death not possible unless a reason was given.

She had to find a way to escape this robot thing before it turned her in to people who would no doubt kill her.

She shook her head and mentally berated herself. She could run of course. Why didn't she do that in the first place?

She tore her eyes off of the robot and dashed away. She heard it coming after her and she ran away quickly.

Where was Jesse?

Why wasn't he helping her out?

Emi heard an odd crunching noise and looked back to see that the robot had somehow changed its shape to become a metallic cheetah. Her heart nearly stopped beating at the sight, but she kept running.

Could she actually die in this program? For instance, if she died in here, would her body die as well? She didn't want to test it out, but it seemed to be getting closer and closer to becoming true. 'Oh why hadn't I thought to question Jesse further before taking this stupid test,' she groaned mentally.

Her eyes happened to spot a curtain drawing back and she frantically gestured for whoever it was to help her out. She saw the person glance once at her and the robot behind her before the curtain was closed once more.

Despair filled her and she stumbled only to feel someone grab her hand. They pulled her forward and she followed. She turned her head and her eyes widened when she saw a person who reminded her of someone she knew.

She couldn't dwell on who that was though, as they were still running from the robot.

He saw her glance and pointed toward an alley up ahead. She nodded, slightly unsure about all of it, but as he seemed to be her only way to escape she'd trust him for now.

They ran into the alley and she followed him as he jumped onto a platform and then over the fence. He led her around for quite some time before he opened a door leading into a warehouse and pulled her in. He immediately closed the door and put his finger to his lips in a gesture for her to be quiet. After a moment, he relaxed and stepped away from the door.

"I appreciate your help, but I don't understand. Why did you help me? This world, this society, it doesn't seem like the kind to have people helping others," Emi said. Not to mention the fact that Jesse had programmed them that way.

"Well, it's true that it isn't," he agreed. "But I would not say that I am fully part of this world."

"Why not?" she asked.

"Because I am not supposed to exist," he explained. "I am a bug in the program."

Her eyes widened as she realized that he was what Jesse had told her to look for. "A bug has to be created though, so you do exist don't you?"

He shook his head. "It is by mistake then, but it does not matter. What does matter is that you must return to where you came from. This world of equality will kill those unaware of its rules."

Emi twitched at the word kill and said, "I don't know how to return though. See, my friend is the reason I'm here and for some reason he hasn't been answering me. I'm not sure why."

"That would be my fault," he said with a sheepish look. "Because you are with me, he cannot see nor hear you."

She stayed silent at that and looked around. This world firmly made its way into her creep-o-meter. It just seemed too much the same, too much equality.

Not to mention it had creepy robots to enforce the rules as well. It seemed entirely too odd.

"I need to get out of here. Is there any way you can help me with that?" Emi asked looking at him.

He shrugged. "It is not a matter of whether I can help or not. It matters whether you wish to go back."

She frowned at what he said. "That doesn't make sense."

"It does though. Your subconscious is the one that is here, therefore if you wish to leave you merely wake up," he said.

"So, I just wake up?" she asked.

He nodded.

Easier said than done, she thought. Her eyes widened as her vision started to fade again. "Wait, what's your name?"

Her last glimpse was of him smiling and then his whispered breath. "It's Jesse."

Emi woke up and blinked as she took in her surroundings. She wasn't in the program anymore that was for sure. She was back... back in her own world.

"So, how was it? I lost you for a bit," Jesse said as he began taking the lines off of her head.

"I hated that world, but I met someone there. Someone whose name is the exact same name as yours, and now that I think about it... looked like you too," she told him.

"Really?" he asked. His eyes widened and he leaned closer to her. He seemed to realize what he was doing and backed away with a shake of his head. "So, that was it. He was the one who made it not right. I see, thank you Emi."

She shook her head and stood up. "Whatever... just don't make me go back in there again. I nearly died, okay."

"You did? Hm... perhaps I should make some modifications to the rules then. Perhaps they're a little too harsh," Jesse commented as he went back to his computer.

"Just a little?" Emi repeated a frown on her face as she stared at him. "I went in there and this robot immediately declares that I'm breaking some rule and I had better justify it or kiss my life goodbye!"

He seemed about to protest, but closed his mouth when she continued.

"Then, as I'm running, I see someone look out their window, but don't even bother helping!" she yelled. She took a deep breath to calm herself down before she went on. "Look Jesse, I know that utopia is a perfect world and all, but perfection just doesn't work. People need a little chaos in order to function. Can you understand that?"

He looked at her silently in contemplation before nodding. "I'll take your advice in consideration."

"So I can stay here then? And take the extra room you have?"

"Yes," Jesse said. He paused as he was about to get back to work on his program. "Do you need help bringing your boxes in?"

Emi blinked in surprise at his offer. He didn't usually go out of his way to help her, at least not for nothing. "That would be nice, thank you."

"It is not a problem," he said and walked over to the door of his lab. He opened it and gestured for Emi to go ahead. "Would you like to go out later to have dinner?"

She froze on her way to the door. "You're being awfully nice, why?"

Jesse looked at her and smiled. "I am proving that perfection works, and therefore utopia does as well."

Emi stared at him aghast. "Did you even listen to what I said?"

"I did, and that is the exact reason why I am taking you to dinner."

For the life of her, she could not figure him out. "Fine, but you're paying."

"That is suitable," Jesse said a smile still on his face. He watched her walk out of the room before he followed her, the door to his lab closing behind him.

Perhaps Emi was right and his Utopia did not work, but he would figure out a way to make it work. And perhaps having her stay at him home would give him inspiration in finding a solution to Utopia.

Love

The town was decked out in pinks and reds. The occasional white could be seen as well. What did all this mean? It meant that Valentine's Day was just around the corner; the day that was a beauty for couples, but a nightmare for Rina Williams.

The reason why? Well, every Valentine's Day she had to suffer through the fact that she had a crush on her best friend, Alec Harfield. That wasn't the worst of it though. The worse was that he was dating her other best friend, Julie Lansing.

How did it end up this way? What deity had she angered to be cursed with loving someone who was taken? She thought back to when she had first met him…

Rina had just moved from California to Oregon. Having finished packing, she had gone to the park. There were few clouds in the sky and she didn't think that it would rain.

She was so wrong.

A few hours after she left it started to rain, and being a California-bred girl, an umbrella wasn't on her person. Immediately she ran for shelter and found a play area with a roof.

The rain didn't appear to be lessening any time soon and she had to get home. Her parents would be worried as she had told them that she would be home by four, and it was nearly 3:30. Rina bounced on her feet trying to think of a way to get home without getting soaked. It was getting to be 3:45 when a voice startled her out of her worried state.

"Hey! You're that girl that just moved in next door to my house aren't you?"

Rina turned around so fast that she got whiplash. Holding an umbrella was a blonde-haired boy with blue eyes that twinkled in amusement. She smiled at him as she glanced at the umbrella longingly. "Yeah, I'm Rina Williams, and you are?"

"Alec Harfield at your service!" he said with a goofy grin. "Need an umbrella? Your parents sent me to find you and help you out with your rainy problem."

Rina blushed in embarrassment that her parents had sent someone after her. They were too overprotective sometimes.

"Yeah, that'd be great. I didn't think it would rain so I neglected to bring an umbrella," she said. She rubbed the back of her head sheepishly.

"Well then, let's get you home. Wouldn't want you to get sick after all," he said cheerfully. Grinning, he took her hand in his and pulled her close to him as he held the umbrella above their heads.

Rina discovered that Alec was a very talkative person. They went from one conversation to another and the next thing she knew they had arrived at the front of her new home. She stood on her porch and watched as he walked away.

"Um, Alec?" she called. "I don't know anyone around here, and if you're not busy…"

He turned around and showed her a big grin. "Sure, your parents and mine hit it off big, so no doubt your parents have my number. Just call me whenever, or since you're just next door… come over."

Rina grinned as well and nodded enthusiastically. "I'll do that!" she yelled to him with a giggle as he walked backwards home. He waved at her with a huge grin on his face before he went into his home.

That was the day they had met and became friends. That day also marked the first time she ever had a crush on someone.

At the moment, Rina was walking to the park where Alec had said to meet. She thought it was sort of odd that he wanted to have a group hangout on Valentine's.

After all, he was in a relationship, so wouldn't it be better for him to spend time with Julie? The thought of that didn't help the feelings she had in her heart though. Rina still liked Julie as one of her best friends, but the jealousy was still there for all that she didn't want it.

Oh well, for whatever reason Alec wanted to hang for she would know soon. The park was only a few blocks away after all.

A frown struck her face as she noticed something peculiar. Everywhere she looked there were roses in every color imaginable. While flowers being out on Valentine's Day weren't unusual; it was the fact that the roses were being offered for free.

Was there some kind of event going on that she didn't know about? Maybe Alec would know... after all, he was the one who paid attention to the events going on in town.

She was in a state of curiosity as she rounded the corner and into the park. As she came closer to the meeting place a shout startled her from her whirling thoughts.

"Hey Rina, over here!" Alec yelled enthusiastically waving his hands in the air.

Grinning at his antics, Rina waved back at him. Drawing closer, she noticed that Julie wasn't there. "Hey Alec, where's Julie?" she asked glancing around at the places Julie would usually be at.

His face twisted slightly and he said, "Julie's sick with the flu. Blegh, I hate getting sick. I feel bad for her. Getting sick, especially on today of all days." He shivered then shook his head. "Okay! We'll enjoy the day for her! Yes, that's what we'll do."

"Speaking of Valentine's Day, is there some kind of event going on?" Rina asked as she walked over to a tree and leaned on it.

"What an excellent question! Of course, an excellent question deserves an excellent answer!" Alec said as he spun around once and posed with one hand on his chest and the other in the air.

"And the answer is?" Rina prompted.

"No doubt on your way here you noticed the roses. Well, couples all over town are using those roses to communicate with each other. It sounded like fun, so naturally I decided we'd do it too," he said with another dramatic pose.

"Naturally," she muttered dryly.

Apparently, Alec had not heard because he continued on. "Hm, we can start off with giving roses to Julie, and then we can give each other a rose. What do you think?" he asked.

"Oh, um, sure," Rina said biting the inside of her cheek. Maybe she could tell him how she felt... and basically say goodbye to their friendship in the process. Still, if she didn't try she wouldn't know. This was the perfect opportunity; if he didn't feel the same way then she could say that she misinterpreted the flower's meaning. Yes, that was what she'd do.

"Well then I'll go get Julie's rose and yours, and then we'll meet at her house," Alec said before running off.

Was it just her, or did he blush when he said he'd get her flower? Rina looked uncertainly at his retreating figure before she ran off as well.

She had to have imagined it. Her overactive imagination was playing tricks on her again.

Rina slowed to a halt in front of a florist who was arranging roses in a vase. "Um, excuse me miss?" Rina asked hesitantly.

"Yes? Are you here for a rose?" she asked turning around.

"Yes, but I'm not sure what color represents friendship," Rina said looking behind the florist at the vast assortments of colors.

She smiled and turned back around. She took two roses and wrapped them individually. She turned back around and handed the first one to Rina. "Yellow stands for friendship, and in olden times, people believed it meant jealousy," she said. With a twinkle in her eye, she gently gave the second rose to Rina. "For the one you love. Thank you for your business, happy Valentine's Day."

Rina smiled gratefully at her before running to Julie's house, the roses hugged gently to her chest.

Julie's house wasn't that far from town. Rina had run all the way there, and she was only panting slightly.

She walked up to the door and knocked lightly, her other hand holding both roses behind her back. The door opened after a moment and Julie herself was there.

"Rina! Hey, how are you?" Julie greeted her voice sounding congested.

"I'm fine," she lied. In reality, she felt like there were a million butterflies in her stomach.

"You're lying," Julie said glaring at Rina with her hazel eyes.

"Why would I lie?" she asked a bit hurriedly.

"Because you wouldn't want to hurt my feelings," Julie answered with a small smile.

Rina didn't say anything. How could she when that was the truth? The only time she ever lied to her friend was when the truth would hurt her feelings.

"Alec told me about the event. So is there anything you want to give me?" Julie asked smiling as she looked at where my hands hid behind my back.

Nodding, Rene brought out the yellow rose from behind her back and gave it to her.

Taking it, Julie held it in both hands. "Did you know that yellow roses meant envy a long time ago?" she asked echoing what the florist had said.

Blue eyes widening in surprise, Rina said quickly, "I didn't mean it that way! I meant—" Rina stopped as she saw her friend shake her head.

"Alec's waiting for you at his secret spot. Go, don't keep him waiting Rina," Julie said giving her a gentle push with one hand, the other still holding the rose.

"I don't understand," Rina said stumbling back a bit.

"You will," Julie said looking wisely. "Now, hurry up and find him."

Still confused, Rina walked off the porch and looked back once before running off again this time to the secret spot that Rina had found Alec at one day. She clutched the rose tightly, but gently at the same time. Its dark hue of red a great contrast to the white shirt she was wearing.

Behind Alec's house and her house was a dense and dark forest. Due to its outlook not many people ventured in. Alec had though and Rina had discovered him there by accident.

She found out that it was his secret spot and she respected his privacy by not intruding. Now she was on her way there and the butterflies kept fluttering.

Rina stopped in front of a weeping willow tree; the entrance to Alec's secret spot. She took several deep breaths before plunging through the branches of the willow tree.

As she came out on the other side she saw Alec sitting on a log holding a rose in his hand. The color was hidden from her sight however. "Alec?" she called to him softly.

He stood up and slowly turned around. The color of the rose was revealed and she stared in confusion at it.

"Rina, you're here," Alec said warmly. Walking forward he suddenly stopped a worried look on his normally chipper one. "About the rose—" he stopped as if he didn't know what to say.

Rina shook her head at him. She showed him her rose from behind her back and spoke up. "How long?"

"From that rainy day," he admitted looking into her eyes.

"Then why did you go out with Julie?" she shouted dealing with her confusion through anger.

"Because she asked me, and I couldn't tell her no," Alec confessed. "I hate hurting my friends, you know that."

Her anger softened when she saw his dismayed look. "But you would be hurting yourself... and me."

He looked at her immediately, his eyes wide in alarm. "I didn't want to! Not intentionally anyway..." he explained hurriedly. He went to his knees as he held his rose out to her. "I'm really sorry Rina, forgive me?"

She considered his pleading expression and the rose in his hand before she nodded. She gave him her rose as she took his. "I forgive you. Happy Valentine's Day."

Alec smiled at her. "You too Rina. Thank you."

Blind Faith

Matt and I have been going out for five years. It seems like a really long time… but it isn't. Simply because I'm not really sure he really loves me. Is one-sided love truly a relationship?

Well, maybe it is if they don't realize it. Except, I know that he doesn't. At least, he hasn't once said 'I love you' to me. I know they're just words, but they mean something to me.

I looked up from my thoughts when I saw him walk by me. "Are you going to work Matt?" I asked.

"Yeah," he said pausing to answer me. He looked back at me, his green eyes giving me a glance before he continued walking.

"Be careful," I called to him. "I love you."

The door opened and then closed.

I closed my eyes and struggled not to let go of the misery I felt. I've tried so many times to get him to say those words, but he always refuses. I don't understand, and I'm starting to feel like I'm the only one in this relationship that wants it to work.

I couldn't understand it. My mother had always told me to respect myself and allow no one to disrespect me without reason. So why was I allowing myself to stay in this relationship?

It hurt, and I was beginning to dislike it.

I decided then; when Matt got back, I was going to find out whether he truly loved me or not. If not, then I would leave.

I couldn't stand being in pain anymore.

With a firm decision in mind, I went into my room and started to put my things into a suitcase. I would be ready for whatever his answer turned out to be.

The door opened and Matt walked through it. His black hair was slightly matted with sweat and he looked tired.

I waited for him in the living room where he would always go to first. He came in and stopped when he saw me. His eyes narrowed at me and I knew he was asking me what I was in there for.

"Matt, there's something I have to ask you," I said quietly.

"What is it?" he asked coming to stand near me.

"Do you love me?"

I watched his reaction and frowned when I saw that he merely blinked.

"I would think the answer to be obvious," Matt said after a moment.

I clenched my fist and looked away from him. "Then why haven't you ever told me so?" I asked my voice quiet, but unwavering.

"I… I can't say," he said and I heard his voice from another direction and figured that he had looked away as well.

"What makes three simple words so hard?" I asked turning my head back to look at him with a small glare.

Matt looked at me and said, "I can't explain okay? What's the reason for all this anyway Sarah?"

"I feel like I'm the only one fully committed to the relationship we have," I said a tone of quiet fury evident in my voice. I stood up but didn't look at him. "I don't want to be with you if I'm the only one in love. I want to share it with someone who actually cares."

"Where are you going with this?" Matt asked quietly as he took a step closer to me.

"I'm leaving, and unless you can give me an actual reason… I'm going and I'm not going to come back," I told him. Tears were starting to form, but I forced them back. I could not cry in front of him, not now.

He stayed silent and I brushed past him. "I guess not. Good-bye Matt," I said before I picked up the suitcase I had left out to the side and walked into the hallway. I opened the door and paused wondering if he was going to stop me. He didn't and tears started to fall from my eyes. I walked out and left him.

Three days. Had it really been three days since I left him? It seemed so long ago, but at the same time like it was just yesterday. I could hardly believe what happened, but I knew that it had occurred. The fact that I was currently staying in a hotel some miles away from the town that I had been living in for so long was one source of proof.

I stared out the window at the falling rain and sighed. Matt and I had met on a day like this, and we had many memories with the associated with it. A stray tear trailed down the side of my face as I remembered the times I spent with him. I did miss him, dearly, but if he didn't love me, what point was there to staying?

There was a part of me that hoped that he would find me though. Matt and I had always been there for each other. He was my silent support, and now he was gone.

I sighed once more, tired of the misery I felt. I was awful with him, and awful without him. There didn't seem to be any balance at all for me.

There was a knock on the door and I frowned. Why was there someone at my door? I didn't send for anyone, and I had already paid for the night, so why?

I briefly entertained the thought that it was Matt before I dashed them. He hadn't stopped me before, why would he be coming for me now?

That thought didn't stop me from hoping though.

I opened the door and my eyes widened when I saw a shirt damp and soaked from the rain. My blue eyes traveled up and I saw green eyes looking into my own with pain, misery, and concern.

"I'm sorry. I do love you Sarah, but I never could say so before. I'm not much of a speaker, and I hate to explain how I feel," Matt said quietly. Water dripped from his black hair as he looked at me with those forlorn eyes. "But I hate coming home to an empty house. I hate having no one to listen to about what happened on the news. I hate not having you in my life. I'm not asking for your forgiveness, but at least let me come back."

I listened to his plea and somewhere inside me started to heal. "I hate not being with you too. I understand now, thank you. I forgive you. It's my fault too for not noticing that you do care," I said softly. Taking his hand, I smiled at him and brushed the wet hair that was stuck to his face. "Come inside, you'll catch sick if you stay in those clothes."

He walked in and I saw that his eyes were filled with love, even if his words weren't.

Everything would be okay, I knew it.

Courage

Pit. Pat. Pit. Pat. The sound of pacing filled the empty hallway of Raybourne High as Riley Carter contemplated a choice that would affect his life. Well, his high school years anyway, or maybe his whole social life. Yes actually, his social life… that sounded a lot better.

His decision would affect his entire social life and if he made the wrong choice – bam! – His life would be over! No more group hang outs, no more study groups, no more classes together, heck with that, no more school! He would be doomed if he made the wrong choice! Doomed!

He wanted to tear his hair out in frustration, but knew that he'd suffer the consequence if he did. Would hitting his head against a wall help any? Maybe, but it would probably only result in making him more of an idiot than he already was.

Riley glanced at the clock and noted that lunch was over in a few minutes, which meant that she would be getting out of class soon as well. Should he tell her? Should he tell the girl that he had a crush on since eighth grade that he liked her? Should he? Would doing so ruin their friendship if she said no? Yes, yes it would! So, why was he even considering it?

He looked at the wall and thought that it might not be so bad to become more of an idiot.

"What are you doing? I hope I haven't made friends with someone who has the potential for lunacy."

Riley spun around mid-step to see his friend, Miranda Trent.

She had just transferred from her old school to here, but he knew her before that. Actually, Miranda was also the person that introduced him to her; Janice Sanders.

He turned his attention back onto Miranda and noticed the amused look on her face. He hurriedly explained to her before she could go and retort with another insult at him.

"I was thinking about… some things," he told her hesitantly. He wasn't sure if he wanted her to know what was going on, given her tendency to insult him. Granted, she might know already given the fact that he was so obvious about it.

Miranda looked at him curiously and tilted her head to the side. "What things?"

Riley wanted to face fault, but straightened up. He forgot; she was pretty much dense in even noticing signs of love. "It's nothing," he said wanting her to leave so he could go back to pacing.

"No, it's not nothing!" she said sharply. "Nothing is something, so spill it!"

"It's really nothing—"

"Liar!" she accused as she pointed at his face.

Riley blinked as he noticed how close her finger was to his eye. If she wasn't careful, she was going to take an eye out.

"Tell me now and I won't annoy you to the ends of the earth," Miranda threatened him.

If he hadn't known her personally, he would have laughed at the fact that Miranda – who was rather short in comparison with other girls – was threatening him. Since he knew her though, it was no laughing matter.

Riley looked around and grabbed her hand. He pulled her over to a secluded spot and looked around once more. Then he started to actually explain to her once he made sure that there was no one listening.

"There's a girl I like, and I want to tell her I like her, but I'm afraid of what could happen—"

"Besides her liking you back and consequently agree to be your girlfriend?" Miranda offered looking at him with her usual amused smile.

"No," Riley said frowning. "If she doesn't like me back, it could ruin our friendship."

"Oh, you're friends with her? Who is it?" Her brown eyes lit up as her curiosity grew.

"You know her," Riley began.

"I do? But I haven't exactly been at this school long enough to make friends—" she protested before she was the one to get interrupted.

"It's Janice," he said in a whisper.

"Huh, Janice?" she repeated. Then her eyes grew wide and her mouth went into an 'o' shape. "Really, you mean…"

"Yes, I do mean her," Riley said his face red.

"Oh," Miranda paused as she remembered all the incidents that should have signaled to her that her friend liked her other friend.

There was that one time that she saw him willingly dance with Janice despite the fact that he couldn't dance. Then when she was sick, Riley had gone over and stayed with her the entire time. There was also the fact that he was always around her.

Miranda thought it over and reminded herself not to mark things off as friendliness just because it looked like it. Her instincts didn't usually ever work around subjects of love.

"So, are you going to tell her?" she asked raising an eyebrow at her friend.

His eyes widened and he yelled, "Haven't you been listening?"

She blinked and took a step back. "Maybe I should leave, you're obviously too upset to talk like a normal person."

Riley looked at his only hope for advice walking away and his heart nearly stopped. "Wait! Don't leave! I'm not upset."

Miranda looked back and smiled. "Oh really? How not upset are you?"

He heard the sly tone in her voice and he paled. She wanted something from him, he could tell.

"I'm so not upset that I'll… buy you a bar of chocolate," he offered hesitantly knowing her penchant for sweet treats.

Miranda tilted her head thoughtfully to the side and considered what he said. After a moment of thought she said, "Nope, not enough. Consider the flavor."

He blanched and scowled. Trust Miranda to try for more. Good thing for her he needed her advice so much, and maybe her help. "Fine, how about white chocolate instead?"

She suddenly swung around and landed an innocent, yet sinister smile on him. "Let's go get that white chocolate bar then! Then I'll give you all the help I can give!"

Riley sighed and followed behind her as she skipped off.

"So, what should I do?"

Miranda put the tip of her finger into her mouth and licked the last remnants of the chocolate off of her finger. She then took it out and inspected the rest of her fingers. All clean… unfortunately. She looked at Riley and said, "Well, you like her right? Enough that eventually it's going to cause fissures in your friendship anyway."

"No it won't," he argued in a stubborn tone.

"Fine, it won't, but still. You can't expect to live your life knowing that you never got up the courage to tell her how you feel. After all, what if later on you see her with someone else, what would you do? Be jealous despite the fact that you have no claim over her?" Miranda asked her voice taking on a tone that signaled him to listen. "You're going to have to tell her."

"I can't, it might ruin our friendship," Riley said with a groan.

"And if it doesn't? Janice isn't the type to let something like that ruin a friendship. She's a decent enough person for that," Miranda told him. She frowned before she suddenly slapped the surface of the table.

Riley jumped and shouted, "What was that for?"

"I had an idea. What? I can't express things by making noise?" she asked looking at him with a raised eyebrow.

"You're an odd person you know that?" he said. "That aside though, what idea do you have?"

"It's real simple actually," she said.

"Well?" he asked after she didn't say anything.

"I'll ask her if she likes you," Miranda said as if it was the most obvious way to go about it.

"What?" Riley nearly yelled but saw a teacher's stern look and quieted down. "Are you insane that's about the same as me confessing!"

"No, because I won't ask her in a way that would insinuate that you like her," she told him before she stood up. "Okay, I'm heading to class now. The bell's going to ring soon."

He looked at the clock and noticed that she was right. "Alright... hey Miranda?"

She stopped and looked back at him. "Yeah Riley?"

"Thanks, and if she does like me, could you tell her I like her back?"

She smiled and nodded. "Will do."

Miranda twirled the feathery pencil in her hand as she sat on her bed. She was currently supposed to be contemplating the idea for her next story, but she couldn't help but think of what to say to her friend.

There were plenty of ways she could go about it, but the one that drew her most was to ask her through elaborate and dramatic ways. She looked at the clock and grimaced. Obviously not enough time to plan something like that.

Guess that left her with her only logical choice left… bluntly. Yes, the best choice was for her to ask Julie if she liked anyone.

(Anyone hopefully being Riley.) Yes, that was her plan.

Miranda placed her pencil down and picked up her cell phone instead. She dialed her friend's number in and waited as the dial tone sounded. Soon her friend's voice filled the receiver and Miranda quickly got into character. Life was after all filled with acting; she may as well act through the phone call as well.

"Hello Janice? It's Miranda," she greeted with a smile in her voice.

"Miranda? Oh! Hi!" Janice greeted back jovially.

"So, how are you?" Miranda asked as she carefully planned out her conversation in her head.

"I'm good. Just watching some good ol' television."

"Nice, oh, I have a question for you," she said as she made herself sound as if she had just thought of the question.

"What is it?" Janice asked.

"Well, the thing is, I'm just curious, but is there anyone you like?" Miranda asked sounding merely curious.

"Um, why do you want to know?" Janice asked after a slight hesitation.

"I told you, I'm curious. What reason else is there?" she asked putting an annoyed tone to her voice.

"Well, there is someone I like…"

Miranda perked up and listened closer. This secret crush thing was easier to find out than she thought it would be. "Who?" she asked her curiosity larger than it was before.

"Riley."

Miranda allowed silence to take over the conversation as she heard her friend's confession.

Janice asked worriedly, "Is everything alright?"

"Oh, oh everything's fine! Riley huh? Riley… as in you really like him?" Miranda asked barely able to keep the glee from her voice.

"Well yeah, I like him," Janice said. Then after a moment she said in a slightly raised voice, "You're not going to tell anyone… or him are you?"

"….No," Miranda answered and the excitement could be heard in her voice.

"You are, aren't you? Miranda, don't be such a jerk!" Janice yelled her pitch rising in her panic.

"Now now, don't be calling people names when they bring good news," Miranda told her in a slightly sing-song voice.

"What good news?" she asked suspiciously.

"Oh well you know, just a mild fact that Riley likes you back," Miranda said casually.

"What?"

"I said Riley liked you back," she repeated.

"I heard you the first time. You aren't lying to me are you?" Janice asked suspicion filling her voice once more.

"Nope, he told me to tell you that he likes you. Well, only if you liked him back anyway," Miranda told her friend.

"Wow, if that's really the case, I just can't believe it," Janice said her voice filling with awe.

"Believe it Janice, because he really does like you," Miranda began. "So, my suggestion is that you tell him the good news… right now."

"Now? But he's not home, he's training," she said knowing that Miranda would understand what she meant.

"Then go there and tell him, the sooner he knows, the sooner the both of you will be all lovey-dovey and happy-like," Miranda told her.

Quiet TV noises could be heard before Janice said, "Thank you Miranda, you always give the advice that's the best. I'll go do that now then. Bye!"

"Bye, good luck!" Miranda said cheering her. "You know he likes you, so have confidence!"

"I will! Bye!" Janice said before she hung up.

Miranda smiled at her phone and looked at the empty page in her notebook. Ideas were coming, and all thanks to a phone call.

"Hey Riley, Janice is here, she says she wants to see you."

Riley nodded and went outside. As he walked he thought of various reasons to why she had come. Had something went wrong? Could it be she wanted to ask him something? Or, could he actually dare to hope that she would say she likes him back? He didn't know but he was hoping.

He saw her and his stomach nervously flipped. Well, it seemed like it did. He was too busy concentrating on not doing something stupid in front of her to notice.

"Riley, hi," Janice greeted once she saw him.

"Hi," he greeted back. "What are you doing here Janice?"

"There's something I want to tell you," she began.

His heart stopped for the second time that day. "What is it?"

A smile burst onto her face and she suddenly tackled him in a hug. He took a step back to stay upright and looked at her bewildered. He then heard three words that nearly made his heart stop a third time.

"I like you," she said into his ear.

Riley stood there holding her shocked and could barely believe what was happening. She had said it. She actually liked him! He mentally shook his head and laughed as he said, "I like you too!"

"Good, because I was beginning to get worried at your silence," Janice joked.

He laughed alongside her and had to wonder why it had seemed like such a problem. Janice actually liked him back and his life wasn't destroyed! He mentally reminded himself to get Miranda another white chocolate bar before he hugged Julie once more. "It's cold outside, want to get some hot chocolate inside?"

"Sure," she said.

They then walked inside holding hands while the full moon steadily rose behind them as if watching over the love that had grew and blossomed.

2009

Umbrella

It was raining. Not the little dribbles you find during summer; no, it was raining as if the entire ocean was being dropped down. Well, either the ocean or some rather large lake. Either way, it was raining like no tomorrow.

Kalie found the rain annoying, yet useful.

There was the fact that the rain made her hair wet. Not to mention it took a while for all of her fur to dry off, being a coyote shape shifter and all. That was the annoying side to the rain though. There was a useful side to it too.

The rain gave the perfect opportunity to use an umbrella.

Kalie's green eyes sparkled in delight as she watched the rain fall in steady drops. She held onto her umbrella tightly as she walked out from the school entrance. Hearing someone call her name, she stopped and turned around, a soft smile playing on her lips.

"Hey Kalie, you weren't really thinking of leaving me behind were you?" Damion asked his red eyes gleeful and mischievous as always. He walked to the edge of where the overhanging cover was and leaned against the railing, his long black hair swaying gently in the wind that accompanied the rain.

"Maybe and what if I was?" she asked. She held out her umbrella for him to come under and pulled it back when he was close.

"Kalie, love! I thought that your heart was mine and mine alone! Why are you doing such a cruel thing to me?" he cried putting a hand over his heart in fake pain.

"It's just a little rain," she told him. She glanced casually around before she smirked at him. "It's not as if a werewolf like you couldn't handle it."

"But... but... I'll be wet," Damion protested. Then it was his turn to smirk as he thought of something. "Alright, but you're the one who will have to deal with the smell of a wet wolf."

Kalie paled before she quickly extended her umbrella over to him. As much as she loved teasing him, she did not like smelling wet canine anything.

Living in a family full of shape shifters and werewolves made her known to the fact that wet canines did not smell entirely good.

Damion walked under her umbrella and leaned down to give her a small kiss on the cheek before his arm snaked around to hold her around the waist. "You know love, there's a tradition that those who share an umbrella are going to be couples, but did you know that the other part of the tradition is that they have to kiss too?"

"You completely made the second part up and at any rate, you already kissed my cheek," Kalie told him.

"Then forgive me for that sin and quickly reprimand me by showing me the correct way," he replied looking at her with a grin.

"Idiot," she told him before she quickly shoved him away from her and out into the rain. "Get your own umbrella!"

"But Kalie love—!"

"Go away Damion, I'm not sharing an umbrella with you and that's final!"

Then again, the rain was more annoying than useful.

A Moment in Time

It was Christmas Eve and snow fell over the town like a large fluffy white blanket. Flashing neon lights from the stores showed that they were still open to last minute shoppers. Very last minute shoppers.

Most people were already home enjoying their Christmas dinner with their family or loved one. There were still a few stragglers around though. One girl in particular, is where this story begins…

Kalie ran out of the store, her deep red hair dropping down to her back. Her green eyes were wide with panic as she looked for another store. She found one, but ran out soon after. It didn't have what she was looking for either.

Collapsing onto a bench, Kalie tilted her head up to the sky. Cold droplets of snow fell onto her face and she closed her eyes as a snowflake nearly fell into it.

Her parents were likely to be enjoying a private dinner, and her brother was likely to have taken his girlfriend (her best friend) to dinner in some fancy restaurant.

Kalie would have been in some fancy restaurant with her boyfriend as well, but she had turned him down saying that she had something to do.

It had hurt to see him looking so sad, but she didn't have a choice. She had already gotten Christmas gifts for everyone but her boyfriend, Damion.

It was certainly horrible of her to wait until the last minute, but he was very hard to choose a gift for.

Her best friend, Talia, had told her to just spend time with him, but Kalie told her that wasn't enough. Her brother, Kite, had just told her to not get anything for him, but then Kite didn't really like who her boyfriend was. Her parents were no help either, they just told her the same thing Talia had.

What could she get him to show that she cared about him? Was there anything at all she could get him?

With eyes closed, Kalie hadn't noticed anyone around her. She did though when the steady fall of snow on her was gone. She opened her eyes and gasped in surprise.

"Damion? What are you doing here?" Kalie asked as she stared at her boyfriend.

He was wearing a casual outfit and his long black hair was in its usual ponytail draped over his shoulder. His blood red eyes were staring into hers with such intensity that a blush arose onto her cheeks. He was holding an umbrella, the reason why the snow had stopped falling on her.

"I was looking for you, love," Damion said. "No one should have to spend their Christmas Eve alone right?"

"I wasn't spending it alone," Kalie protested. "I was looking for something."

"Oh?" He raised an eyebrow curiously. "And what would this something be?"

"Nothing," she said tight-lipped.

"Nothing is something love. Tell me what it is please. Tell me what's so important that you didn't want to spend Christmas Eve with your boyfriend," Damion said leaning in close to hear her answer.

Kalie bit her lip as she tried to think of an answer. She sighed and unclenched her hands that she had unconsciously clenched. Damion deserved better than a lie. There really was no point lying to him. "I… I was looking for a present to give to you."

"A present for me?" A smile broke onto his face and he chuckled lightly. "Kalie love, getting able to spend time with you is enough for me."

"Really?" Kalie asked.

"Yep," he answered.

The bells from the clock tower suddenly rang for midnight startling the both of them.

Damion chuckled and pointed to the top of his umbrella where a mistletoe could be seen hanging. "Merry Christmas Kalie," he said leaning in further.

"Merry Christmas Damion," Kalie said and closed the gap between them.

Light snow fell over the two like a soft veil. Fireflies blinked on and off around them giving a magical feeling over the scene. It seemed to be nature's gift to the two.

Damion then suddenly leaned back and commented, "A one-way trip to Canada would be nice though."

"Damion!" Kalie scolded as she lightly hit him on the arm.

"What? Canada has a lot of open space," Damion said smirking. "Can I be faulted for wanting to spend my life with the girl I love in a place where few people can bother us?"

"No, I guess not. Although, you might want to wait a few years before going through with that. We're not exactly done with our schooling years after all," she said as she put her hand in his.

"Of course," Damion said as a smile appeared on his face that was only for her.

Smiling back, Kalie walked away with Damion beside her. He was her love, and her Christmas present, just like she was his.

Nothing could ever change that.

Sin

'Twas the eyes that drew me in
Of crimson gold and liquid fire,
Then born was a love of sin

I asked for a cup of gin
And my heart was set afire.
As I saw the eyes that drew me in

I must have died in that grin
Thousand times over, she I would admire
Could this be a love of sin?

Disregard the voice of my kin
Be the situation dire,
Can't forget the eyes that drew me in

Had I never seen her grin
Never would I have gone higher
That fateful day was a love of sin

When did this love truly begin?
What was love, and what was desire?
Twas the eyes that drew me in
And born was a love of sin

Tipsy

It was decidedly a boring day, Maron thought as she went about her usual Sunday morning activities. It was like most weekend mornings: rise, eat, do chores, and lounge around. She felt perfectly content to just lean back into the couch as she flipped channels randomly.

Her mother did not feel the same.

With a single command, Maron was sent off of her comfortable seat and on her way to the front door to get some fresh air, as her mother had so dearly thought she needed. It was as she was passing the window next to the door that she found a reason to neglect her mother's order.

"Mom, there's a raccoon in front of our door."

Her mother looked up from her knitting with a raised eyebrow, but set her project down upon the expression on Maron's face. She made her way to where her daughter stood staring out the window and a quiet gasp of astonishment escaped from her. "It's staring at our door… isn't it?" she asked her voice just above a whisper.

Maron had the time to wonder whether her mother was talking in a hushed voice so as to not scare the raccoon or because she was in such awe. She shrugged mentally and decided that she didn't care for the answer.

There was presently something of more interest to her, and it was staring at her front door with a loopy grin on its face. At least it looked like a grin, of which if it was, was definitely loopy.

She had to wonder if it was alright, when she noticed the traces of berries on the raccoon's face. "Is it drunk off of berries?" Maron pondered out loud.

As if to prove that, the raccoon slowly turned around. Its gait reminded her of a drunken man and she watched with amusement as it ambled off.

She laughed as she saw exactly the way it moved. The raccoon's back legs appeared to be going just fine at their swift speed, but it was the front legs that were the major source of amusement for her. They seemed to be dragging and the entire image of the raccoon running off with its face practically in the ground was too much for her to handle. Maron was soon on the floor holding her sides as gales of laughter burst from her.

Her mother stayed standing as she watched the raccoon stumble away. She soon looked down at her daughter and gave a quiet chuckle. "That raccoon will be regretting those berries in the morning," she said grinning.

"Yeah, I'll bet," Maron agreed looking out the window. She grinned as well and found it amusing that her Sunday morning turned out to be not so boring after all. The only thing she regretted was that she hadn't gotten a picture of the incident.

But, perhaps if she was lucky, the raccoon would eat the berries again. Then her often boring day would become more interesting than before.

She could only hope.

Treasured

It was my heart you took that wintry day.
A day when the clouds were ever present
And the cool ground covered in lush white
snow.

I happened to meet your eyes and your smile,
Full of love directed only at me.
My breath was lost to me upon the sight.

Those sweet and tender words you spoke to
me,
Even now I hear them as clear as day.
For the words I'd spoken then are still true.

Will you listen to me as I have you?
Will you say those precious words of 'I do'?
Or will I be left alone on that stand?

For I hope you know, that my love for you
Will always remain my most treasured
love.

2010

Obsessed

The sliding doors to the supermarket opened as the two of us approached it. I grabbed a cart as I walked through the doors. I glanced back to see Shelby behind me. She was staring at the white sheet of paper that she had written the things she needed to buy on it. She looked over to me and gestured to the fresh food area.

"I'm going to need… celery, cabbage, and carrots," Shelby listed pointing out each vegetable with her hand as she leaned on one of her crutches.

I gathered the items she had asked for and placed each in their own plastic filmy bag. As I placed them in the cart, I looked at her with a semi-serious scowl.

"Why couldn't you have just ordered this stuff online? It's not like they wouldn't have delivered it fresh."

"Sean, humor me. I go grocery shopping every Sunday regardless of any broken limbs," she said smiling at me as she waved a hand at the blue cast on her leg. "It's a tradition, be thankful that I'm including you in it."

"Sure it is… you just want someone to hold your stuff," I told her with a teasing grin.

"Technically, the cart is holding my stuff," Shelby replied.

"Well then technically, I'm driving it."

It was her turn to scowl as she stopped, resting her weight on her good leg as she waved a crutch at me. "Oh do you always have to win the argument? Don't answer that!" she said hurriedly when I opened my mouth to speak. "Let's just hurry up so I can go home and watch my soap operas."

"Because that is so important," I said grinning. I grabbed the list from her hand and moved off towards the next item. I passed by the apples as I went to grab some pears. I took my time finding good ones, knowing that Shelby would get further annoyed with me.

"Excuse me."

I heard the small whispered warning before I was bumped aside. I turned back with a bewildered stare to see a young lady stacking the apples in a pyramid shape. Having finished her task, she hurriedly walked off.

"Okay... does she work here?" I asked watching the girl place items into her own cart and then immediately straighten out the shelf from which she had taken something. "Or just have an issue with disorder?"

"The latter," Shelby replied. "She goes grocery shopping every other Sunday, likely due to the fact that it's a stressful matter to her."

"So... a case of OCD..." I murmured continuing to watch her.

"Oh no, don't you dare do what I know you're thinking of!" she said sternly. "That girl probably won't like your interfering with her, and she probably wouldn't appreciate it either! Just save yourself the trouble and forget her."

"You know I can't do that," I said my mind already trying to figure out a way to help her overcome her problem. "If I see someone in trouble, and I can help them… I will."

"And how do you propose to do that?"

"Just watch me," I said before I pushed the cart to a few ways in front of her. I picked up a can of fruit and looked at it thoughtfully before setting it in a different place than before. I moved forward and refrained from smiling when I heard her make a small noise of complaint. I did the same thing as before, except with a can of beans. Once more she fixed it after I moved away. On the fourth time, she placed the item back a little forcefully before tapping me on the shoulder.

"Excuse me, but could you please stop that? If you're not going to get something, then put it back where it belongs!" she said her voice rising in her annoyance.

"Sorry, but what's the point of that? It's put back either way, isn't it?"

"That's not the point! Look, just don't do it again please," she pleaded before she directed her cart around mine and hurried away.

"So your plan is to annoy her to insanity?" Shelby asked as she made her way over to me.

"Of course not, I'm just getting her used to the idea of disorder," I replied.

"Stupid, there's a reason why it's called OCD. There's no room for disorder in that world," she said as she shook her head.

"I'll make it fit, now what else was on your list?"

"Sean! I don't see you for weeks and suddenly I see you at the grocery store? What's going on?"

I sighed and turned around to face my oldest friend. "I've been busy," I said with a shrug of my shoulders.

"Does this have anything to do with that girl? Cause if it does, so help me, I will smack you with these crutches!" she warned threateningly.

I held up my hands in front of me as she waved said items. "Now wait, hear me out before you go all samurai on me. She's changed, thanks to yours truly."

Shelby placed her crutches back on the ground as she stared at me incredulously. "You're kidding, right?"

"Nope, the girl's genuinely changed. See, look over there," I said pointing over to the produce section.

The girl from before who had such trouble with disorder was intentionally putting things in disorder. Apple pyramids were left topless, stacked oranges would be un-stacked, and various other items were placed differently from where they were.

Shelby stared at her with a frown on her face. "You actually did it? How?"

I grinned at her and flashed a thumb up sign in the direction of the produce area when the girl glanced at me. She smiled softly before going back to her shopping.

"It's called persistence, and lots of it. She was obsessed with putting things in order, so I helped her to become obsessed with putting things in disorder. I figure that it's an easier issue to resolve from."

"You're crazy Sean… nice, but crazy," Shelby said shaking her head.

"I just have to help people if they need it," I said smiling. "Call it my obsession."

Victory

All was still up above while
White wisps and puffy clouds
adorn the sky.
A glint of green and a moment later
A dragon of the deepest emerald
appears!
Bursting from the cloud, blue flame
in its wake,
The dragon roars and announces its
arrival.
The people far below can scarcely
believe their eyes,
For a creature of that size had never
been seen.
They flee and scream as the dragon
approaches.

Grown men who had gone to battle pick up their spears,
Despite knowing that they would be going towards certain death.
Children crying as they run from their mothers,
Furry little pets cower in their hiding spaces,
And all is panic as the dragon nears the ground,
Until a flash from the sun reflects off of a shield.
A knight has come with victory in his eyes!
He raises his sword as the dragon roars.
His shield is raised as flames burst forth.

The battle lasts for hours,
Or perhaps it was minutes,
The people knew not,
For when the dust had cleared, the victor was certain
The green dragon lay on the ground, death in its eyes,
And the knight stood victoriously over the lizard.
The people cheered and danced
And they knew then that they would always remember…
The day that the knight vanquished the dragon.

Dangerous Territory

She was so tired of being her friends' designated driver all the time. Just because they wanted to go drink their heads off didn't mean that she wanted to drive them to and fro. Granted, she would rather drive them than hear that they died, but still… didn't they know when to stop partying?

And those pulsing lights and music, it was driving her nuts! Maybe she was just tired… physically, mentally, emotionally, whatever. At any rate, fresh air would do her good, so with a signal to one of her more sober friends, she walked out of the club.

She closed her eyes as she took in the air and a smile lit on her lips. Yeah, fresh air was definitely what she needed.

A minute had passed before she turned around to go back inside and froze when she saw a pair of glowing red eyes from the alleyway. She didn't have a chance to scream before she was grabbed and pulled in. A dark resonating chuckle was all she heard before everything went black.

Liana's cell phone buzzed and rang beside her bed. She opened her eyes and grabbed it glancing at the name once before putting it to her ear. "There had better be a good reason for calling me at this hour Damion, or you're going to be finding yourself running on two paws," she growled. The sun hadn't even set yet for crying out loud!

"It is a good reason, and it's not exactly like I could wait a few hours for the sun to leave before I called you. It's too important for that," he said.

Liana perked up slightly as she heard the grim tone to his voice. Even if it was a dangerous situation, her friend/lackey would always be able to shed a light of humor into a situation. "What's happened?" she asked getting out of bed. She went over to her closet and quickly grabbed an outfit. She didn't know what was going on, but likely she would need to be around.

"They found a girl in the side alley of the club—"

"She's not dead is she?" Liana interrupted. Her green eyes widened and she froze as she waited for his reply.

"No, not dead, but it was a close one. Cops found her when someone called in anonymously about there being a body near the club. Thing is Liana… she was nearly drained," Damion said. "The cops want to talk to those who worked at the club last night, and the police chief wants to speak to you too."

"Fine, at the club?" she asked holding the phone to her ear through her telepathic abilities alone as she swiftly changed into the outfit she had picked earlier. Maybe it was someone who got turned without a mentor to help them out, or perhaps the attacker was a rogue. She frowned at the thought. A rogue would be a serious matter, and measures would have to be taken in order to keep her town safe.

"Yeah, and Liana?"

"What?" She paused as she was putting on a black silk-like glove.

"There's this guy wearing a suit, and apparently he's here on official business. Janet looked into his mind and apparently he's here to make sure that the town fits into the state's laws. So I'd be careful about what you say when you talk to the cops," Damion said.

"East Valley has been up for this long and they decide to send someone to check up on us now?" she snarled into the phone as objects in the room floated into the air in her anger. "And if we don't fulfill these laws, what then? Do they shut us down? What right do they have?"

"Liana, calm down. I'm just warning you so that you don't end up blowing up when you get here," he said calmly. "I'm sure they have a good reason for choosing to check up on us now. So let's not run with assumptions that just might get us into trouble."

She stared at the floating objects in her room in silence before they slowly drifted back to where they were before. "When did you become the voice of reason huh?" the vampire asked her werewolf friend in amusement. "I'll see you in ten, no, five minutes."

"Don't go chasing any squirrels now," Damion said chuckling.

"As if," Liana replied before she grabbed her phone and promptly hung up. She put it into the pocket of her jacket and grabbed the rest of her things before going over to her door.

She gave a quick check for people before pulling on her shape shifting ability to turn into a form of a wolf. She dropped to the ground just as soft, sleek black fur covered her body. Seconds later, she shook her head and a toothy smile shown on face. It didn't matter how old she got, she loved being able to shift into any form. Of course, being able to avoid getting roasted in the sun was also a bonus.

Liana slowed to a stop and peered at her club from the bush she was hiding in. She counted four police cars and two other cars that belonged to the investigative unit of the police. She gave the cops a cursory glance before she trekked over to the back.

Damion was waiting by the door when she shifted to herself. His long black hair was tied back in his usual style, and his red eyes looked uncharacteristically grim. He managed a weak smile upon seeing her. "You know… if not for the fact that you drink blood, people might think you're a werewolf when you're always shifting into a wolf," he commented as he held the door open for her.

"You know, if not for the fact that you squander away your time in the sun, people might think you're a vampire with those red eyes of yours," Liana responded with a smirk at him.

"If they do, they don't care. The girls love me all the same," Damion replied smirking as well.

"But you don't love them back, even a smidgen… right?"

Liana chuckled as Damion quickly went over and got to his knees in front of a girl with shoulder-length red hair. Her hands were on her hips as she stared down at her boyfriend with fiery green eyes.

"Of course not, love! After all my heart beats only for you!" Damion declared as he held her hands.

Kalie grinned and pulled him to his feet. "If you were any other guy… I would have smacked you for that corny phrase."

"Ah, but if I were any other guy… I'd be dead," he said wryly. "Your brother's got a protective streak a mile wide, he'd kill anyone just for breathing near you."

"And yet… you're still alive," she said raising an eyebrow at him.

"It helps that I'm your brother's best friend," Damion said with a devilish smirk.

"Guys… semi-dead body, cops in my club?" Liana reminded them. They looked apologetically at her and she shrugged off the look as she walked past them. She moved into the main room of her club and saw most of her employees sitting around. They looked over to her when they noticed her walk in. She gave each of them a reassuring glance before she noticed Julie, a young girl with pixie blood, being interrogated by one of the cops.

"Can you remember anything else from last night?" the brown-haired cop asked with a stern look of suspicion in his eyes.

"No, I've told you already! I went to work and nothing unusual happened," Julie told him anger swimming in the depths of her eyes.

"Excuse me officer, but I believe that you're harassing my employee," Liana said placing a hand on Julie's shoulder after having walked over. "Julie, why don't you go ahead and pour some refreshments for everyone?"

She nodded stiffly and walked over to the bar. Liana turned her attention back to the cop and withheld a smirk at his livid look. "Is something the matter?"

"You just interrupted a police investigation, you do realize that is a capital offence and I can have you arrested for that?" he warned threateningly.

"I also realize that harassment is also an offence and I could put you on citizen's arrest," she responded back allowing her smirk to surface.

"I know what you are, you and all your fanged workers," the cop hissed. "I—"

"Now just hold off on your accusation," Liana said her green eyes glinting in warning. She noticed Janet to the side of her vision stand up in obvious anger.

Knowing that it was likely something the cop had thought and that the psychic was not easily angered unless she had heard something directed towards those she cared for, Liana figured it was an ill thought towards her.

"For one thing, not everyone that works for me is a vampire," she started and her sharp eyes noticed his flinch. "Sir… perhaps you have had a bad experience with vampires in the past, but if you are an officer of the law, you are not to bring your personal feelings and prejudice into the matter. Continue to confront those under my protection with your false accusations and I will make sure that your career as an officer is over."

He was physically shaking as Liana turned around and abruptly left him. She made her way through the stools and tables over to the blonde haired psychic. "You look upset, was what he said that bad?"

Janet nodded and tightly gripped the front of her dress. "He accused you of being that girl's murderer, and he also accused you of other murders in the city. As if you were even there in the first place!"

Liana could only smile as she saw the younger girl seething in anger. "I could understand myself being upset at having heard that, but you don't have to get upset over it for my sake. Any of you," she added having seen Julie about to protest from behind Janet. "We have a larger issue at hand after all. I'd like for everyone to stay here while I get the cops and that one person to leave. There are things that need to be discussed without them listening. Damion, you're in charge of making sure the cops in here don't harass anyone else until I get back."

"Got it," the werewolf said and continued to lean against the wall as he stared at the cops in the room with a predatory look. Kalie sat on a stool next to him and she also began to stare at them. As if by signal, the rest of her employees went to watching the cops.

Liana chuckled under her breath when she walked by a cop who had his back turned from the bar and kept glancing back with paranoia covering him like a jacket.

Leave it to her faithful employees to make a goal of putting the cops through a bout of fear.

The police chief was standing next to the door looking out the side window when Liana approached. For a moment, neither spoke until the chief broke the silence.

"I have your word that the attack was from an unknown?" Silvia asked not looking away from the window.

"You do," Liana said also looking out the window to the fading sunlight. "They all knew the rules when they signed on to work here. If any of them disobeyed, I would know."

"I trust you; after all you care for this town as much as I do," she said turning to look at Liana. Her look was serious as her voice went low. "The girl we found was nearly drained dry. There weren't any marks to indicate that she had been bitten, but perhaps they had been healed…"

"Then if they were, we would be dealing with a rogue," the black haired vampire said grimly.

"A rogue… in my town?" Silvia growled and golden eyes behind sunglasses suddenly flashed in anger.

"Excuse me, but I believe you mean our town. I will not allow for a rogue to traverse unattended either," Liana said watching the sun leave with satisfaction. "It will be night soon… Silvia, you should get your people to find out who's been coming in recently."

"I will get on that, and what will you do?" the wolf shape shifter asked.

"I'm going hunting of course," Liana replied a fanged smirk playing upon her face. She turned around and paused as a memory came to her. "Two things, Silvia…"

"Yes?"

"One of your cops has a prejudice against vamps, the brown haired one with a scar on his neck. You might want to watch out for him. With his attitude and behavior, he is going to get himself into trouble one day. With me, possibly, if he continues to harass people around me," Liana said as she watched the cop mentioned. Her eyes narrowed as she saw him speak to a peppermint-scented man wearing a suit. "Silvia, do you know that man?"

The police chief looked over to where Liana was staring at and her own eyes narrowed. "He's the so-called inspector of the town neighboring ours. I don't trust him, but he's got official papers stating who he is. All the same, he makes my fur itch."

"He hasn't even spoken to me and I don't trust him," Liana said. She saw him look her way and she adjusted herself to appear friendly.

He spoke a single thing to the cop before he walked over to her. "So I am told that you are the owner of this establishment?" he asked. "I'm Perry Lindstrom, inspector from the town near yours."

"That's not very specific," she said raising an eyebrow.

"It's a rather private town. We've heard of the special circumstances of the people living here and we thought it would be a good idea to extend a welcome hand," Perry explained.

"Extend a welcome hand? And that requires an official inspector like you?" Liana asked keeping her tone pleasant despite her growing anger. He obviously knew of East Valley and its not necessarily normal inhabitants, so what exactly was he doing here? "And what if the town does not pass this inspection of yours? What will you do?"

Perry shrugged his shoulders and waved his hands about him. "What happens will happen, but if this place does not fulfill criteria then it will simply be made to fit."

"And you have the authority for that?" Silvia asked.

"Ah the police chief, yes, I do have the authority. I am the official inspector after all," he said his smile wide. "Well the day is getting late and I must be getting to inspect before it grows too dark."

"Leave a number we can contact you with before you go," Silvia instructed.

Perry continued to smile, though it seemed a bit perfect. "I have already done that with one of your officers. Good day."

Liana watched him leave the café before she turned to Silvia with a growl. "He's not just untrustworthy; he's a sleazy slime ball too!"

"I have similar thoughts," Silvia said. "But as of now there is nothing we can do. If he proves to be dangerous to us then we'll deal with him then. Agreed?"

The vampire nodded before she abruptly turned around and headed over to the bar. It was time to get this hunt started. "Damion, Kalie, you two are coming with me. Janet, you're in charge and make sure everything goes alright during club hours," she instructed.

"Right." Damion and Kalie looked at each other before they moved from their spot and went to stand by Liana's side.

Silvia raised her hand and made a gesture. Seeing the signal, her officers came over to her. "Okay listen up everyone, the club's opening soon and when that happens we're going to be blasted by noise and sweat. So get what you need and move on out! And Thomas, quit harassing the employees. You're a cop not an interrogator!"

"It's so nice having the chief be one of us," Damion commented in a whisper to his girlfriend.

"Quiet, the normal cops might hear and think you mean something else," Liana warned in a low tone.

He looked somewhat apologetically at her before he held an arm around Kalie's waist, waiting for the moment that the cops would leave.

Slowly they trickled out and Silvia nodded at Liana once before she left as well. Moments later, they heard the sound of cars driving away.

"So the cops are gone, where are we off to?" Damion asked.

"The back alley where the girl was attacked," Liana answered. She glanced at the window and smirked when she saw the last edges of the sun. "Time to go."

They made their way out of the club through the side door. Liana stood at the entrance of the alley, silently observing it. There wasn't much to see aside from the various junk. Scent-wise… there were drops of blood that smelled human and had to be from the girl that was attacked. None from her attacker, but she had expected that. A rogue would not be careless enough to spill his own blood.

"Hm… not much to see," Damion observed.

"I agree there isn't much to see, but what about our other senses?" Kalie suggested before she shifted into a coyote after having made sure no one was watching. She nudged Damion with a wolfish grin before she moved past him into the alley. He followed after her with a watchful eye.

The coyote pushed aside trash as she looked for any clues that would lead them to the attacker. Minutes passed before she gave a sharp yip, her paws scraping away the surrounding trash.

"What did you find Kalie?" Damion asked as he kneeled down next to her. He picked up the object she gestured at and frowned as he stared at it. "It's a piece of handkerchief… that has a metallic scent…"

"Let me see," Liana said. She took the object from his hand and stared at it. It was a single torn white handkerchief, but the scent on it was definitely of blood. She held it to her nose and closed her eyes as she took in the scent. Something familiar about it...

"Of course!" she gasped her eyes wide in remembrance. She gripped the cloth tightly in her hand as she looked out of the alley. "I knew that he wasn't to be trusted, but to also return to the scene of the crime? It's like he's intentionally calling attention."

"What do you mean? Who is it?" Damion asked looking at her with a frown.

"Not to be trusted?" Kalie asked after having shifted back. She stood up and placed a hand on Damion's arm as she had a thought. "You mean that inspector guy?"

"I do. Peppermint cloaked him earlier, so I figure that he must use it as a way to disguise his usual scent," Liana explained. "He laid out something of his that would be found by anyone with a good nose."

"He's challenging us?" Damion suggested.

Kalie looked at him with a confused expression. "But why would he do that? What would he gain by challenging us?"

"Earlier when I spoke to him, he said that he knew of East Valley, and that he wanted to lend a helping hand," Liana said her eyes narrowed as she recalled the meeting. "It is almost as if he's testing us…"

"He said he was from a town near ours. Could he be from a place that's like East Valley?" Damion asked looking at her.

"Perhaps, and if he is, we had best show that we are not to be messed with," the vampire said showing her fangs as she looked at the rising moon. "Come my lackeys, let's go look for this rogue before he strikes someone else of our town."

"Don't call us lackeys!" Kalie and Damion both yelled.

"You work under me, therefore you're my lackeys," she replied laughing. She pulled out her cell phone as she quickly walked out of the alley. "I need the two of you to keep a nose out for peppermint. I'm going to call Silvia to tell her what we found out."

"Right."

Liana dialed Silvia's number as she continued walking. A moment later, a black wolf and a red coyote appeared on either side of her. She smirked as the stern voice of the police chief came through the phone. "Silvia, there's some news I think you should know…"

The police chief closed her cell phone and gripped it tightly as she looked around the room. "Who here has the phone number to the inspector?" she barked out in a loud voice.

"Thomas does," offered up one of her officers, Nick. "But he ran out about fifteen minutes ago."

"Where?" Silvia asked looking at him.

"I don't know Chief," he said shaking his head. "He was muttering about justice or something and then ran out."

"And no one stopped him?" she growled. "I want his location found and reported to me in five minutes! Get on it!"

Silvia slammed her hand onto the table for emphasis before she went back into her office. The unfortunate side of being the police chief was that she couldn't go after anyone without information and a reason to go. She envied Liana for that; the vampire had the freedom to hunt.

She was sitting at her desk carving into a bone when a firm knocking came at her door. She put the carving down as the door opened and a head peeked through the opening.

"Chief, Thomas wouldn't answer his cell, but I was able to find him," he said walking fully inside.

"Well then where is he? I want a location, not a drawn out explanation!" Silvia snapped narrowing her eyes at him.

"He's at East Park!"

"Then get our people there!" Silvia ordered as she stood up.

"On it, Chief!" The young police officer nodded at her before he hurried out.

Silvia smiled as she walked out of her office in a brisk pace. She may miss the freedom to hunt, but the power she held was thrilling as well.

"So, Thomas is it? You've explained to me that you don't believe that your town fits the bill. But the way that you explained it is rather confusing. I'm not quite sure I understand."

Thomas nervously wringed his hands as he stared at the tall imposing inspector, of whom he was beginning to regret calling.

The man had on a loose-fitting suit and he wore dark sunglasses, odd considering that the sun had already set. Perry was looking at him expectantly though, so it was too late to turn back.

"This is going to be hard to believe, but the reason is that there are vampires living here," Thomas said quickly before he could change his mind. "It sounds crazy, but it's true! You have to call whoever you work for and get them to rid this town of those leeches!"

Perry's expression didn't seem to change even after the officer's outburst. After a moment of silent watching, he smiled slowly.

"Leeches you say… perhaps they are just living here?" he asked.

"Living here?" Thomas repeated with a scoff. The memory of his parents being murdered before his eyes and the scar on his neck made him bold as his voice grew louder. "More like those leeches are just lying in wait to kill their next victim! They're disgusting things that shouldn't even exist!"

"Is that so?"

The warning tone to Perry's voice didn't register to Thomas as he nodded. "So will you get rid of those creatures?"

"Of course," the inspector said his hand reaching up to grip his sunglasses. He lifted his sunglasses off of his face as he smiled cruelly at the officer. "And the first creature I see is right in front of me."

Thomas found himself frozen as he stared into red eyes. "You… you're one of them?" he gasped.

"Oh yes, I'm one of those disgusting leeches. I am curious as to why you haven't died yet though. With a mouth as foul as yours… anyone less than me would have killed you outright. Perhaps I should carve out that mouth… right before I drain you…" Perry trailed off as he tapped the officer's face with a look of bloodlust in his eyes. He stopped his movement towards Thomas' neck when growling came from behind him.

"Perry Lindstrom. I knew there was a reason why I didn't like you…"

"Liana… how quaint… Have you come to share this thing with me?" he asked turning around slowly to look at her, not even glancing at the two canines by her side. "Oh right, you don't bother with fresh blood anymore. It's all that packaged stuff isn't it?"

"Let go of the human," Liana ordered.

"Or what? You'll sic those dogs on me? Please, I am not afraid of any mutts," Perry declared reaching behind him to grip Thomas' throat tightly.

"What about bullets sent straight to your head? I'm sure not even you can survive that," Silvia said as she approached with her gun aimed at Perry. "Unhand my cop now."

Perry's eyes narrowed as he looked from Liana to Silvia and the police officers that had come with her. "You protect your town well," he acknowledged letting his eyes rest on Liana.

She stared at him with a steely look to her eyes as Kalie and Damion continued growling. "I am not the only one who protects it," she said. "I say once more... release him. Your kind is not welcome here and failure to obey the laws is death."

"My kind? Have you forgotten that you are also like me?" the rogue asked smiling snidely at her.

"I was under the impression that you place yourself in a different category what with your manner of eating after all," Liana replied.

Perry still smiled as his hand tightened, and at the same time Silvia took a step closer. He glanced at her and then at the terrified face of Thomas. "Well then… this has been an interesting experience. Be assured… we will see each other again Liana," he said looking at her. He suddenly pushed Thomas towards Silvia and left in the blink of an eye.

Damion made to go after him, but Liana pulled him back. "No, he's already gone. You would be wasting your energy looking for him," she told the werewolf. She turned to Silvia and smiled tiredly at her. "How's the cop with the attitude problem?"

Silvia placed him on the ground gently and looked up at her question. "Thomas is fine. He's just knocked out from the fear. I'll have a talk with him about his attitude later," she said. She stood up and made a motion to her officers. They nodded at her before going off. Her look was solemn as she stared at her long time friend. "Liana… do you know why he was here?"

The vampire frowned slightly as she thought it over. "I have a guess… Kalie, Damion, what are your opinions?"

The two of them looked around before they shifted back. Kalie was the first to speak after having stretched.

"It seemed to me like he was just testing us… no, testing you."

"If he was a rogue though, to what would he gain by doing that?" Silvia asked.

Damion tapped his foot on the ground as he pondered it. "What if…" he started and trailed off as he continued thinking.

"What is it Damion?" Kalie asked looking at him.

His eyes were closed as he spoke again. "What if he was here because he heard of how East Valley was started? I mean... we all know the real founders of this place, and it's not the humans in the text books. What if he was here to find out why exactly a couple of vampires would make a town with the intention of allowing humans and vampires to co-exist?"

"But East Valley has been around for years now. Why would he come now?" Kalie asked.

"To get that answer we would have to know more about him, but likely what he told us before is false," Silvia said contemplatively. "Let us leave this case closed. I believe that the three of you are wanted at a certain club...?"

Liana smiled. "Yes in fact, after all we don't have a body in the back of the club and Janet is likely wanting a release from temporary manager duties. Kalie, Damion, go ahead and help out with that please."

"Okay, will do," Kalie replied grinning. She waved at her boss and the police chief before running off in the direction of the club.

"Well... are you going with her?" Liana asked with a raised eyebrow at the werewolf.

"Don't take too long out here. We need you at the club too," he said frowning at her. He looked at her for a moment longer before he followed his girlfriend.

Liana watched him leave and turned back to look at Silvia when she made a small noise. "What?"

"It's kind of cute how they care for you. I saw earlier when your employees were intimidating my officers. They kept telling me how they hope they never have to do a case there again," Silvia said with a small chuckle. She looked at the vampire and narrowed her eyes at the far-off look. "You're going to hunt for that rogue still, aren't you?"

She nodded solemnly. "If he's left East Valley then I'll stick to a simple patrol. I don't want to allow for a chance for anyone else to be hurt because of a rogue or another creature coming here."

"Are you sure about doing this on your own?" Silvia asked concern in her eyes.

Liana patted her on the shoulder with a smile on her face. "I can take care of myself. And I won't be long. I have a club to watch over after all," she said. She started backing away and waved her hand once at the wolf shifter before disappearing into the shadows.

"Nick," Silvia said after she was sure the vampire had left.

"Yes?" He walked over to her side and stood at attention.

"Tell the others that they're free for the rest of the night, and if anyone needs me they'll have to wait until tomorrow," she told her officer.

"You're going with Liana to find the rogue?" Nick asked.

"I'm going on my own. If I happen to see her then yes," Silvia replied. "Take care of everyone."

He nodded and watched as she shifted. She wagged her tail once at him before she ran off. She was soon out of his sight and he pushed a hand through his hair.

He had more things to do, and not even the conclusion to another event in East Valley would stop them. "Still, what an interesting event this was..."

Price

"He is going to die."

The vase slipped from my fingers and only a spell previously cast prevented it from breaking. It landed harmlessly on the ground as I hurried to my sister. "How Cassandra... show me how he dies."

She looked at me solemnly, unshed tears sparkling in her eyes. Without saying a word, she lifted her hand to touch my own.

I closed my eyes as Cassandra shared her vision with me. A man with unruly brown hair stood in front of two children, an expression of fierce contempt directed at the white-haired man standing in front of him. I recognized the kids as Quinn and Caitlin,

David's children: the man standing in front of them... and the man that was fated to die. He pulled a sword out from his sheathe as the man before him held around twin swords. As if by signal the two attacked, their swords singing as they struck.

David seemed to be handling himself well, even against two swords. Then another person came onto the scene, a sword in his hand as well, and the tide of battle turned.

Facing against the three swords, David was losing. He had more injuries than the other two combined. The white-haired man suddenly went for the children, and in the moment that David went to save them... the third attacker chose that moment to strike him down.

I stumbled back from the intensity of the vision, and in doing so broke the connection my sister had made with me. I looked at her with tears in my own eyes. "We can't let him die… not when we still owe him a life debt after he had saved our lives before!" I declared.

"But in doing so we would be changing the future," Cassandra pointed out softly. "The price for doing that would be high."

"The price for changing the future will always be high," I told her closing my eyes in frustration. "That cannot be avoided."

"But because we are the ones to be changing it, the price will fall to us," she said her eyes closing as well.

"Not us... me," I said suddenly. I opened my eyes as she opened hers. Determination shone through my eyes as I stared at her. "The people need your visions. My visions only give glimpses into what won't happen."

Cassandra was suddenly quiet and her eyes were unfocused as she had a vision. With a broken sob, she stumbled over to hug me tightly. "No... if you go... you'll never be able to come back..." she cried.

I froze as I heard her words. I would never be able to go back home, or... see my sister again? Was saving David worth losing all of that?

I looked at Cassandra's shaking form as her tears soaked the front of my shirt. I did not want to lose her, but I did not want to lose David either. I had made him a promise after all; a promise to return the life that he had given me.

"I'm sorry Cassandra…" I said quietly. I gripped her shoulders gently as I pulled her away from me. "To save his life, I will pay that price."

Tears flowed down her face as she stared at me. "Then go with my blessings, my sister."

I smiled sadly at her before I walked over to a mirror hanging on the wall, and created a portal that would take me to David with the power I had. I stepped through without hesitation even as the portal closed behind me. The price to change the future, to save a life, was paid.

Shape-Shifting

All was silent as I walked through the hallways of my teacher's magic school. It was a large castle that could fit many people, but only six were currently living there. Of those, there was my teacher, his four other students, and me.

I was also the only girl living there as well.

It was because of this fact that I was sneaking through the hallways at night. Markus, my magic teacher, frowned highly upon any of his students being out past curfew. He didn't want his rest to be disturbed by a problem that was due to a mistake.

In normal circumstances I would try to follow the rules, but I didn't have a chance of keeping up with my studies if I let a little thing like that pull me down.

See, I could not rest during the day. The other students took it upon themselves to make sure I could keep up with the rest of them. That meant I was constantly being pelted with spells when my teacher wasn't looking.

They called it preparing me for the harshness of the world. I called it their stupid idea of male superiority.

I would try to pay attention during teaching sessions, but I always was unfortunate enough to have the front seat. I couldn't relax for even a moment because I was constantly on alert for an attack from behind. I couldn't complain to my teacher because he was more likely to think that I could not keep up with the rest of the students and had to make up excuses.

Usually I would stay in my room to study the books I had borrowed from Markus' library. He had an extensive collection that went from simple mundane spells to complex ones.

The other night I had come across a spell that allowed for the caster to speak to all animals. I had a feeling that if I adjusted it slightly, I could change it to allow the caster to shape-shift into an animal.

Transfiguration was Type A in complexity, but I was sure that I could do it. Plus, it might get those boys off my back if I turned one of them turned into a shrew.

The problem was that the only way to practice the spell without being found was to go into the practicing room, which kept magic from being sensed.

The other problem was the fact that Markus' room was across from the practicing room. He was also a light sleeper, which made sneaking around very difficult.

I had to exercise all my skills as a former thief to get inside without a sound being made.

The door closed behind me with only the slightest of noise, and I went still as I listened for any sign of my teacher or the other students. I sighed mentally in relief before I crept into the next room.

I went through another door and closed it as silently as I could. Then, before I could forget, I murmured a spell underneath my breath to block the sound from escaping outside of the room.

The silencing spell was one of the first that I had learned, and one that I used quite often during my night studies. I would be able to hear outside, but no one would be able to hear me.

I pulled out the copy of the spell that I had transcribed onto a sheet of parchment and sat down with it in front of me. I looked it over and made sure that I had adjusted everything that had changed from the original. After I was satisfied with how it looked, I stood up and started breathing deeply in preparation.

All spells involved a method in gathering the magic. The more complex the spell, the more magic was needed. Simple spells required little more than a touch or a whisper of words. The spell I was about to cast involved much more than that.

My hands drew a series of gestures in the air as I began to speak in a soft, but firm voice. I was leaving a trail of magic with my hands and the words I spoke made the glowing path brighter.

The light was blinding as I came to the end of the spell. As I spoke the last word and made the last symbol in the air, I could feel all the magic centering over me. Then as quick as it had enveloped me, it left in the span of a breath.

I blinked in surprise and examined myself. I still looked the same and didn't feel different at all.

Had the spell not worked?

That couldn't be the case. I had looked over it at least a dozen times. There was no reason for it not to work. Perhaps I had forgotten a word in the spell or a gesture...

I was about to try again when I heard a sound from in the hallway. The first door to the practice room opened and I froze.

My silencing spell would not help hide me from sight, and I was still standing out in the open!

I found a hiding place just as the door opened. My teacher walked through with a scrutinizing look to his grey eyes. He glanced around and stared straight at a creamy sheet on the ground.

I closed my eyes in frustration as I realized my mistake. Of all the things to leave on the ground, it had to be the spell I was working on.

I heard the door close once more and opened my eyes to see that Markus had left, along with my spell. I couldn't do anything about it now, and the only thing left to do was go back and try to get some sleep before everyone else woke up.

With a resigned sigh, I pushed away from the wall and headed back to my room.

Breakfast time at the castle started early and ended early. I made my way to the dining hall and saw that I was the first to arrive. I took my accustomed seat by the fireplace, and waited for everyone to arrive.

My teacher was the first and I stared at him as he approached me. He looked at me silently with steely eyes before he turned away.

"Meet me in my office after breakfast," Markus said before he briskly walked off to his seat.

My mind was whirling with possibilities of what he wanted me for as I turned my gaze over to the table in front of me blankly.

It had to be about the spell. After all, what else could it be? The other students wouldn't have a reason to get up in the middle of the night to practice magic, and my handwriting was all over the parchment.

Could he want to talk about the spell itself? Or perhaps he was going to punish me for staying up past curfew, and then practicing magic when I shouldn't be.

What if he didn't teach me anymore? What if he didn't allow me to stay? I couldn't leave; I had nowhere else to go! I refused to go back to living on the streets as a petty thief!

The anxiety left my stomach churning and the thought of eating made me sick. I stood up and made my way over to my teacher.

"I'm not hungry, so I'll be waiting in your office," I told him. I turned around to walk out when he spoke to me.

"I'm not going to accommodate you," Markus said snidely. "Just because you have an upset stomach does not mean that I will shorten my own breakfast to keep you from waiting."

"I don't expect you to," I replied simply before I continued walking with my head held high. Even if I was going off to await my sentence, I refused to show any signs of it affecting me.

I passed by the other students as I walked through the entrance to the hallway. They didn't look at me and I repeated the favor.

I didn't care to deal with their antics this early and I had something else more pressing to worry about.

I had been pacing my teacher's office for the last ten minutes when the door behind me opened.

"Do quit that. You look like a wolf trapped in a cage."

I stared at him even as I continued. "Sorry, I can't help it," I told him as he moved past me to his desk. He sat down and I stopped pacing to stand in front of him. "Look, I'm not going to apologize for what I did, but please don't kick me out. I don't have anywhere else to go."

"Sakura."

I stared at him as he leaned his chin on the palm of his hand.

"I am not kicking you out, nor do I appreciate apologies," Markus said his gaze stern. He gestured to a sheet of parchment on his desk with his free hand. "I wanted to discuss that with you. The original spell wasn't meant to be changed, but you did it anyway. What were you trying to do?"

"I wanted to make a spell that allowed the caster to shape shift, but it didn't work," I explained.

"Are you sure?" he asked with a raised eyebrow.

"Nothing happened afterwards," I said. "So yes, I'm sure."

"You are wrong." His gaze now looked at me condescendingly. "Something did happen, just not perhaps in the way you expected."

I looked at him in confusion. "Markus sir, explain please."

He stood up and walked over to me. He towered a good foot taller and I frowned as he continued to stare at me silently.

"What?" I asked.

"You're glaring at me."

"No I'm not," I said immediately.

He suddenly waved his hand in front of my face and I backed up tense. He raised an eyebrow at my reaction as he took a step back himself, his gaze not on my eyes anymore.

I found myself relaxing and blinked in surprise. "What was that?"

"That…" Markus pushed his fingers through his brown hair as he stared to the side of me. "… Was the first sign of the spell having done something."

My eyebrows furrowed as I thought over what he meant. "What do involuntary actions have to do with shape shifting?"

"Not a lot… if it were true shape shifting. The spell that you cast likely gave you the ability to do that, but you were also changed in a different way," he explained. "You're not completely human anymore Sakura. Whatever the other half is, it has instincts of a predator, or you wouldn't have reacted the way you did before."

"Is there a way for me to change back?" I asked slightly alarmed. I wasn't entirely human anymore? If I had known what would result from the spell, I wouldn't have tried it at all!

Markus looked over the parchment and I held my breath as I waited for him to speak. He looked up and my shoulders slumped as I saw the look on his face.

"I'm afraid not, but I'm sure that this will not affect your life too badly," he assured me in an unusual soft tone. "In fact, it may be better for you."

"How can being half of some animal be better?" I asked not quite understanding.

"You'll find out," he said simply. "Now go get ready for class, and inform me if anything odd happens."

"Thank you," I said. I nodded before I walked out of his office and headed towards my room. Before I could reach it, I found myself being slammed into the wall by a spell.

"Oh look at that, the little witch tripped into the wall. You really should watch where you're going," said one of my daily tormentors. He looked at me with cruel eyes and laughed as I struggled against the invisible bindings.

"Let go of me now Tyson," I growled. I couldn't get rid of the binding spell without the use of my hands, of which were bound. If I hadn't been so distracted, I never would have been caught by his third-rate spell.

"Now why would I do that? I think it suits you," he said looking over me. He leaned close to me with a leer on his face as his hand reached for me.

Something came over me as his hand touched my skin. The bindings seemed to slide off as I pushed Tyson away from me.

He slammed to the ground and I didn't give thought to my newfound strength as I brought my hands together.

They shone with a shimmery glow as I spoke a rapid string of words. The now blinding light left my hands and traveled to Tyson. He tried to crawl away from it, but the light reached him before he could move.

It faded and I stepped closer to him. Tyson lay on the ground and stared at me with an expression of fear in his eyes.

"What are you?" he asked trembling as he tried to inch away from me.

I was aware of the crowd that had gathered in the hallway and saw Markus standing near the back of the students.

I couldn't see what had happened to me, but somehow I just knew what had occurred. I looked at Tyson and allowed a smirk to grace my face.

"Me? I'm a witch, a half-fox shape shifting witch that just took away your ability to use magic," I told him. My gaze was steely as I glared at him. "You will never be able to hurt anyone else with your magic again."

I turned and left through the awed group of students. My new furry triangular-shaped ears twitched at every sound I heard, although most of what I heard was gasps of fear or awe. I passed by my teacher and paused to speak to him.

"I guess you were right… it is for the better," I acknowledged smiling at him.

He rolled his eyes and shrugged. "So you're more confident now. I'm still down one student."

"I'm sure you'll survive," I teased.

"I blame you, now get to class," Markus growled. "I have a former student to get rid of."

I mock bowed to him before I continued walking off.

I wasn't sure whether my new confidence and attitude was entirely because of the fox half, but I wasn't going to think much on it. Things were now a lot more interesting, and I wasn't going to waste it by over thinking matters.

Plus, I had accomplished the spell that I had set out to cast, even if it had unexpected results. Everything was going to be so much better now, I was sure of it.

About the Author

A writer of fantasy, Sasha Nguyen creates stories in the comfort of her own home in Oregon. She was born in the United States on the 24th of September in 1991. She has dipped her hands into various genres, but prefers writing stories that involve humor, fantasy, adventure, romance, mystery, drama, or a combination of them all. She is a dreamer that strives to put her dreams to life.

Made in the USA
Charleston, SC
21 March 2010